MW00593311

An Eye for an Eye

Chronicles of an Obsession

A. Venger

VANTAGE PRESS
New York / Los Angeles / Chicago

CONTENTS

PROLOGUE

I'm an old man now, living alone with a dog. My active life is over, spent, and there is not much time left until the always-sneaky entrance of the great extinguisher. So I am in a hurry. I want to tell this story before his coming and my going.

I'm not a writer, really, and have no literary pretensions. I lack the skill, imagination, and creativity to conjure tales out of my hat. This is the first, last, and only one ever to be produced by me, so I do hope it is worth telling and that someone will be out there, listening.

Not possessing a writer's wit does not preclude credits in other fields, though. I am fairly well educated, intelligent, of the straight line, analytical kind. I am also well read, reasonably honest, at home in seven languages, and, until late in life, possessed of preposterous good looks, of the boyish, dark, romantic Gregory Peck type. Throughout my life women have been attracted to me, often embarrassing my inborn shyness.

If this sounds conceited or even narcissistic, let me add that while it is surely a pleasant advantage to be burdened with all these, still it is never more than a starter, balancing out its own effects by turning you careless and lazy.

Anyway, like everything else in this story, it is the simple truth. It all happened as I am going to write it down. No alterations, no cosmetics to make it appear more interesting. Reality is wild enough.

The need for anonymity though, in order not to endanger myself needlessly, has forced some immaterial changes upon me.

A vagueness here, a false clue there, but never anything of importance to the unfolding of the story itself.

I have to protect myself if ever your curiosity should be aroused as to the identities of those figures moving around in the following landscapes. So do not try to detect me, reader, because you won't succeed.

And most important of all, I'm not important at all. I made no dent on history. Quite the contrary is true.

An Eye for an Eye

CHILDHOOD IN GERMANY

My ancestry is buried somewhere in that great mass of Eastern European Jewry, living out their poor and pious lives in the small villages and towns of Russia and Poland, until their destruction in the code-named final solution during the second of the great wars of the worlds.

Some half a century before their oblivion, millions of these Jews tried to run from their future fate by wandering to the west. Pausing here, settling there, most made the great escape to the shores of the United States.

My parents were part of that stream too, but unfortunately did not run far enough. After serving the Kaiser during their Austrian episode in the first of the great wars, they settled in a gray, drab German mining town, opening a clothing store, what else? A painting in our living room, picturing my father in resplendent corporal's uniform, with a fleshwound at his throat to show for his war service, still appears before my eyes. How his service was rewarded, twenty years and another corporal later, can easily be guessed.

I was born in the Roaring Twenties, as the cliché goes describing those years. In a depressed German mining town there was nothing *roaring* to grow up in, I can assure you! Mass unemployment, hyperinflation, streetfights on the left and on the right, Jew-hating and Jew-baiting all around.

Item

I am running in the street as fast as I can and a little bully is hotly pursuing me. I might have been eight and my pursuer ten.

He is running faster, catching up, and will get at me any minute now. Nobody pays any attention, nor will anyone come to my rescue.

Suddenly I swing around and bang my fist in his face with all my might. The little bully is thrown flat on the street and right under a passing motorcycle.

For a split second the world stops dead in its tracks. Then, first as in slow motion, but quickly accelerating, a commotion starts wherein I manage to disappear.

Item

I am cornered in a street by some thug, beating me up while shouting a then popular denigrating anti-semitic street rhyme: *Jude itzig Nase spitzig Augen eckig Aschloch dreckig*. No sense translating nonsense.

The remarkable thing here is not the scene itself, but the typical indifference of the bystanders—everybody going about his business as usual, not paying any attention, much less intervening. As if a grown man beating up a child in the streets should be a part of the normal street scene, like a vendor selling his wares.

Now don't jump to the conclusion that my childhood years in Germany consisted of nothing but street beatings. Far from it. I led a happy and sheltered life in a typical closely knit Jewish family. I remember many pleasant events at home, at school, or even playing in the streets.

There were wonderful birthday parties, outings in beautiful forests, fairy-tale boat rides on the Rhine, visits to relatives in foreign countries—everything a little boy could wish for.

The anti-semitic incidents and occasional beatings did not really hurt me. The physical pain was soon gone and forgotten, and the marks on my self-esteem were compensated by a growing perception of my basic Jewish identity, even dignity. As I did not possess religious inclinations, I became an early, convinced and ardent Zionist.

But real pain and probably lasting harm to my young and sensitive soul was brought about by two unrelated incidents, both ensuing from unintended and thoughtless human stupidity—one at school from my teacher and one at home from our maid.

Let's start with the maid.

Now I happen to have but the fondest recollections of this fair young country maiden for she took me sometimes into her bed and it was there that I first encountered the female anatomy under her willing guidance.

But one night, when I was about nine, instead of the usual playing around, she started telling stories about devils and demons, scary tales probably heard in the village she came from.

One frightened me particularly. It was about some unbelieving student, climbing by nightfall a so-called haunted wall in a dark forest, daring the evil spirits. And sure enough, exactly at midnight he was seen as if he were in the clutches of something invisible, screaming, "He got me! He got me," and was found next morning strangled to death with claw marks on his throat.

Until that night of story telling I was just an ordinary boy, happy-go-lucky like your next door neighbor's kid. But from that evening and forever after, I was scared of the dark and midnight became an obsession.

The second incident happened at school. Like count-less other children in countless other classes we, too, had our exercise books examined by the teacher and returned the next day with her rating marks on a scale of one to ten, written underneath. Now I sometimes had the habit of tracing the digits with a pencil for no particular reason than innocent childish behavior.

One morning the teacher entered the clasroom and assembled all the kids around her. With much dramatising she exposed the "forgery" I purportedly had perpetrated by trying to "upgrade" her marks.

I was terribly hurt, being humiliated in front of all the children, and wrongly accused of something I had not done, nor even intended to do.

But I did not deny the accusation. I just stood there as if paralyzed while the injustice choked my throat. In-stead of defending myself then and there, I started to cry, and when prodded about my tears, I lied and blamed some boy for pinching me, which the poor kid of course denied. So I had become a liar, too.

And until my dying day I cannot understand or explain this inability to stand up for myself and speak out the truth, not even afterwards to my parents.

I often believe that I could have developed into another and better person if this minor mishap had not befallen me.

When I was about ten, the little corporal with the funny moustache succeeded in grabbing power in Ger-many. So we loaded our belongings on a truck and de-parted for another country.

Alas, not far enough, again.

ADOLESCENCE IN ANTWERPEN

Of man's four seasons, childhood, adolescence, manhood, and old age, only the first and third might be of some interest to others. So I will not bore the reader more than necessary with my years of adolescence.

Antwerpen, my new hometown, was known for its large Jewish community. We settled right next to the Jewish quarter with close and closely knit relatives living all around. While adjusting to my new surroundings without much difficulties, I started my new life, easily centered on home, family, friends, and school. As I grew older and developed into an excellent and handsome high school student, girls started to swing into my orbit and the first school romances blossomed and withered away again.

I can still picture the high school theatre where we performed the *Miser* by Molière before our proud parents, myself playing the part of the young lover. I still remember nostalgically our farewell school party, when rhymes were read about each student. Mine was, in Flemish: *Schaakt de meisjes en de stukken, zal in't leven niet mislukken,* which means, "carries off the girls as well as the (chess) pieces and will not fail in life," referring to my abilities both as a chess player and as a Don Juan.

I seemed to have everything going for me.

However, two dark and somehow interconnected shadows loomed over the horizon: The deteriorating economic situation and the approaching threat of war.

Upon our arrival in Antwerpen my father started an agency for various German products. But with the advance of the Nazis, more and more German firms could not or would not maintain a Jewish agent, and finally the whole business frittered away. So back we were in the clothing store, only second hand ones this time.

It was at the peak of the Great Depression and we fell on very hard times. Often there was literally nothing left to eat at home. Sometimes even Friday evenings passed on an empty stomach with my mother blessing the Sabbath candles on a bare table, weeping silently.

Only much later, when they were long gone, did I realize how wretched they must have felt then. My father, the provider, unable to provide life's basics for his family, and my mother, having to see her family go hungry and her child leave home without food.

Because hungry or not, off I went every Friday night, visiting a friend's home, trying to arrive early enough so as to chance on a piece of delicious homemade kiggel at the end of their Sabbath meal. Without ever disclosing, of course, that this cake was my only stomach filler for that entire evening.

My father used to blame our deplorable situation on bad luck—and on Aunt Anna, my mother's maiden sister from Poland who lived with us during those years. In his frustration he took it out on that poor soul and many a nasty scene occurred wherein he reproached my mother for the bad spell her sister had wrought upon our house.

But there were more aspects to life with auntie. As we were living in very cramped quarters, all three, my parents and my aunt, slept in one large double bed. One night I heard very distinctively my aunt's voice exclaiming: "This is an attack I cannot withstand!" So I came to understand that there were other kinds of fights, too.

After some years Aunt Anna returned to Poland. For a while we sent her parcels of used clothes until she was swallowed by the tides of war and disappeared forever.

As I grew older, Zionism got an even stronger hold on me. Though not being religious, even something of a nonbeliever, I was very conscious of my Jewishness and my belonging to the Jewish people. As I saw it, the root cause of all our troubles and vulnerability was the anomaly of our being a separate people without being a sovereign nation, having a land of our own, just like everybody else. So in my mind the solution was clear and simple: All the dispersed Jews should abandon their respective host countries and return to the historic land of their ancestors, the cradle of their religion and nationhood from biblical times—that tiny stretch of sand on the Mediterranean shores then known as Palestine, a British mandate explicitly designated by the League of Nations to be a Jewish National Home.

This was the classical Herzlian equation. All opposing forces—Arab resistence, British obstruction, and Jewish complacency must be overcome. In my eyes, our needs as well as our rights must prevail.

The only other plausible choice, as I saw it then, was for us to assimilate individually into various other cultures and countries, provided of course they allow you to, intermarry, and in time disappear as a separate Jewish entity. Indeed, many have taken that road in the past, and many more are taking it now, bringing about sooner or later their own private Jewish extinction.

I could never grasp nor agree with the pathetic alternative of the Jewish schizophrenic, trying to preserve his Jewish identity while singing another people's anthem. That's not for keeps! Being Jewish means more than practicing just another religion, or belonging to some esoteric fan club. If continuously evaded, the inevitable choice will be made by others—most probably by a next generation.

I never fathomed another possible road to the final solution of the Jewish problem: to perish collectively in terminal ovens.

My father had been a lifelong Zionist too. A certificate of his inscription in the golden book of the Jewish National Fund, offered by the movement in that German mining town, hung proudly on our wall. However, he was never able to realise his aspirations. In those years there were only two ways of obtaining a certificate, issued by the British administration for emigration to Palestine—either as a youth after years of agricultural training, or as a "capitalist" with a substantial amount of available funds. And as things stood, both roads were closed for us.

How often have I imagined the good life we would have led if somehow we could have managed to reach that land of hope and sunshine, all of us, before the hunting season started in Europe! As a matter of fact, some of my parents' best friends from their Zionist circle had made it, so why could we not have succeeded—all of us together?

But what's the use of daydreaming. It did not come about. And so, one day in May, long columns of German soldiers entered the town, and now it had become too late. We were caught in a ruthless grinding machine out to get us all.

The trap was shut.

WAR

Crowds lined the streets when the Germans came marching in. The first rows consisted of cheering sympathisers and fellow travelers, raising their hands in the Nazi salute. Behind those traitors-to-be were rows and rows of curious onlookers watching silently the long procession of soldiers, trucks and armoured vehicles. There were no disturbances of any kind, everything passed off very orderly and correctly. Probably, most people were relieved that their war was over and resigned themselves to a temporary, correctly conducted, perhaps even benign occupation.

I was there, too, not wanting to miss the momentous event, though not grasping its future ominous impact. I always possessed a reckless streak stemming less from inborn courage than from the frivolity of youth. While looking on, I overheard an obviously Jewish man reassuring his wife: "This may be bad for the German Jews, but not for us. Oh no. They would not dare to touch us. We are Belgian citizens."

Indeed, it looked very much that way in the beginning. They did not even bother any Jews at all—at first. Their master plan to exterminate the Jews was based on deceitfully hiding the hideous end until the end was already there. It was phased out in three separate stages: first, registration, then segregation, and ultimately deportation to the sites of the final solution.

Meanwhile, between each new regulation and the next, they would cunningly instill illusionary hopes that the worst was over and no more troubles lay ahead. But then, all of a sudden, another alarming decree was pasted on the walls. And so it went on—intimidating, frightening decrees one day, sheer acts of terror the next—step by step ever more tightening the screws down the programmed road until the inevitable grand finale in the ditches and gas chambers of Eastern Europe.

The first stage, registration, was perhaps the most important one. It was made to appear purposely as insignificant as possible, and with good cause. It was the cornerstone of the other stages and elementary to their success. Contrary to most East European Jewry, we in the west were not outwardly distinguishable, nor living in separate villages and ghettos. So first of all we had to be found out. If, at this embryonic stage, their plan could have been foiled, their final solution would have come to nothing. But it was not done, nor even attempted.

So no atrocities marked the registration stage, and after just a couple of months, with the cooperation of all concerned including the Jewish community and their leaders, we had our identification cards stamped with a *J* and our names and addresses neatly filed away in the devil's cabinet for future reference and use. And a very near future indeed!

Once the registration was done with, essentially it was all over. The rest was ruthless application of logistics. For all practical purposes, we Jews had become, unknowingly, a bunch of walking corpses.

The second phase was then set in motion—the segregation. All links and remnants of links with the gentile surroundings were successively severed. The cancer had to be isolated.

Signs began to appear in shops, swimming pools, coffee-houses, park benches: barred for Jews, *fur Juden verboten, voor Joden verboden, interdit aux Juifs.*

10

We turned in radios, bicycles, cars, and all means of transportation. Jews were fired from public offices, Jewish doctors and lawyers were barred from having gentile clients. Jewish children were transferred to separate schools, Jewish businesses were appropriated. Food stores served Jews on special hours, and Jews rode public transportation on back seats only. And so on and so forth, in an endless stream of segregatory ordinations.

Internally our pariah society bravely tried to maintain a semblance of normal community life. We had our own schools, stores, newspaper, and a Jewish Council acting as the go-between vis-a-vis the occupying power to represent our interests—or so we thought. We even had our own theatre where outstanding Jewish artists, barred elsewhere, performed nightly before sold-out audiences, and succeeded, believe it or not, in making us laugh our heads off.

But in our hearts, we became ever more scared. The gloves were off now. From time to time, alternately with decrees and regulations, also ruthless acts of terror were perpetrated, serving both to prevent, as to avenge sporadic acts of resistance. In one of those I had my first close encounter with certain death.

One day the Germans surrounded the Jewish Quarter and hounded some five hundred young Jewish males into trucks as retaliation for a previous anti-German incident. As a matter of fact, this was their first large-scale so-called *razzia*, wherein Jews were dragged forcibly from their homes for deportation.

The youngsters caught were sent to a concentration camp in Germany, and within a few months their parents received condolence letters from the authorities, regretting having to inform them that their son had succumbed from pneumonia, or some other disease, and would they please come for the ashes especially sent in urns for their parent's consolation.

Incredible the length the Nazis would go to in their efforts of concealment.

That afternoon I returned home from a Zionist meeting where we discussed the moral dilemma of those engaged in the activities of the Jewish Council. (Conclusion: Total negation.) In passing the Jewish Quarter I saw crowds milling around and German units, called green police, occupying street corners. So, somewhat carelessly, I went in to have a closer look.

I entered a narrow and empty street and at the first corner a German S.S. officer came running towards me, shouting and pistol-waving for me to come over. "Are you a Jew?" he yelled, which I affirmed. By now, another German S.S. trooper had appeared from a side street, escorting five or six young Jewish males on their way to a truck at the end of that street. I was ordered to join in.

The stupidity of my reckless curiosity began to dawn on me, as I saw how group after group of Jews were being loaded into trucks. When we were about half way, the second S.S. trooper came over to me, trailing at the end of our line, and enquired about my age. He then ordered me to get the hell out of there, which I did at once, only to be ambushed at the corner again by the first German, the wild one, furiously yelling at me to get back to the group, who by now had nearly reached the other end where the trucks were being loaded. But this time I did not move, obstinately countering that the other German had sent me away. Then he turned suddenly and ran after them, and I turned around, too, running in the other direction towards a crowd which had assembled at the corner watching us, and they pushed me quickly out of sight, and I kept running and running and running until I reached home.

[That night the first seed was planted inside myself of a harrassing question that has tormented my soul in many a sleepless night throughout all of my later life: *Why me? Why was I spared?* Until, so many years later, I suddenly saw the light.]

Those were the darkest days. Today, with the knowledge and hindsight of history past, it is not so easy anymore to comprehend the abyss of hopelessness and despair of those summer months in 1942, when the only apparent future left for doomed mankind was *1984* forever.

Europe seemed irretrievably lost. The German armies had swept all resisting states from the map with shattering ease—like a knife cutting through butter. The invasion of Russia in June 1941 had resulted in only more of the same. The number of prisoners grew to many millions as they continued destroying and capturing opposing armies. And when the Japanese joined in by attacking Pearl Harbor, surrender followed surrender, spreading general collapse of the democracies worldwide. The whole world seemed now inevitably lost and gone forever.

Strangely enough, the one grace and consolation was a voice from heaven.

Sometimes, in dark nights, they would come over. It would start as a faint humming from the west, rapidly growing louder and louder, and then enormous light beams would rise high in the sky, searching for the intruders. Loud outbursts of big guns would join the noise, already dimming, and eventually disappearing towards the east, until total silence and darkness had returned and the whole event seemed but a dream.

But I would lie awake during those nights, tensely waiting for the occurrence to happen, and when it did it was like heaven, like music from the spheres, an apparition from the beyond.

So it was really, really true. Somewhere out there a world still existed, proud and unconquered, and valiantly fighting back. And even if unattainable as life in outer space, it was real and it was here and had just passed over my very head. In spite of the light beams and the guns, we were not alone, and perhaps not yet entirely lost and forgotten.

Now is as good as ever to disclose this basic deficiency of my lower nature: I never felt one single twinge of compassion, one tiny pang of pity for the havoc wrought by those heavenly invaders upon the German civilian population, doubtless at least partially innocent. Which is but an understatement. The plain truth is that I lay there awake looking at the light beams and listening to the humming above and the explosions around and relished the thought of those German towns, burning.

Once I saw a UFO. I was looking up in the blue sky, as I so often did, and then I saw a white, as if pencilled, line. There was no plane in sight, no clouds, no noises, nothing. It moved one way, changed directions with snakelike movements, and then suddenly disappeared. For whatever reason or connection, I became overwhelmed by a powerful feeling, nay, a certainty, that the current nightmare would end some day with the destruction of the now seemingly so triumphant evil forces.

Then, sometime in the middle of 1942, the yellow star of David was decreed to be sewn on all our outer clothing. After having been filed and isolated, we were now being stamped. At last, the third and final stage could be set in motion. The Jews were now to be shipped out to destinations unknown.

MY LONGEST DAY

By now I have to take the hardest hurdle of this tale and tell about the day I died. This may sound incredible, but the very day of my escape from our common fate—when I kind of seemed to receive a new lease on life—that was the day that started my demise.

[*You are the dead*, the voice said. And Winston knew it was true.]

No Orwellian voice had spoken to me behind a picture on the wall. But that day, even if I did not know it then, lasts ever longer, burns ever stronger, until it will have finally brought me down, and I mean deep down.

I was only nineteen then, in 1942. The previous year I had finished Jewish high school with flying colours. We had passed the examinations with all the attached fuss like all the other kids in the country. As if we still had a future left to prepare for. As if we had not already been blue-printed for choking till death shall follow. Never, ever will I cease to wonder at that surrealistic pretense of going through the motions of normalcy, while all the time the violent end was preplanned right from the beginning.

For a year or so, universities being barred for Jews, I studied civil engineering with the help of gentile students, but most of the time I hung around with the "the group." That's how we called ourselves, divided equally into four boys and four girls, though not in four pairs. Our goal was to found a new kibbutz in Palestine, and in order not to distract our endeavours from this goal, we decided that pairing off was out of bounds.

15

The adult reader surely smiles at our adolescent ideas. Indeed, it did not take long to find out how those holy vows of celibacy were being broken right under my naive and unsuspecting eyes. Though disappointed, the main idea of the group survived, even if not all of its members.

Then, when summer got hotter, rumours started to circulate about the impending deportation of young Jews to labour camps in Germany. Stage three was about to begin.

A plan took shape within our family to organize a collective escape attempt for the younger generation, who were now being endangered. The instinctive distrust of the so-called workcamps must be attributed to our East European, pogram-wise origins and memories. Moreover, I am convinced that it also shows the superiority of intuition over rationality as the real meaning behind those cover words was rationally truly unthinkable.

Indeed, most of those young Jews, now soon to be summoned, really believed the labour camp story, venturing that the work might be strenuous, but they were young and would endure. And eventually they would present themselves at the railway station, carrying the exactly prescribed luggage, for the midnight trains to their oblivion.

The organisation of our escape attempt was in the hands of the elder and more moneyed members of the family, myself being the "contribution" of my parents, whose financial situation had lately eased, somewhat.

And so the day arrived, a sunny Sunday in July 1942, that my mother sewed an amount of dollars in my pants, that I ripped off my yellow star of David, and set out for the railway station. An uncle followed at a distance to report to my parents if I had made it safely to the station, at least. He himself had four children, but had not allowed even one of them to join us, fearful of the dangers ahead.

That was the last day I ever saw my parents. They would live for one more year, and I would be orphaned for the rest of my life.

Nobody knew it of course, on that day. With hindsight it might appear that I had saved myself and abandoned my father and mother to their bitter fate. However, hindsight is so easy, so convenient—in hindsight.

It certainly did not look that way at the time when nothing was known of what we know now. My father had procured a job with the Jewish administration, a minor one, but as such it provided my family a certain degree of temporary security—false security of course. There, hindsight again!

As a matter of fact, on the very morning of my departure, my father, having second thoughts and fears about the escape attempt, succeeded in obtaining one for myself. This job might be a safer alternative for evading those workcamps in Germany than the dangerous journey I was about to undertake. I had to decide immediately, it was up to me.

Some choice to have to make at a moment's notice for a boy of nineteen! But I did. Between staying home with the at least apparent security—false as it proved later on— of a minor Jewish council job, and the perilous journey ahead through closed and closely guarded borders, I made the then more dangerous looking choice. So I bid farewell to my parents and left for the train, and my last image as I left home was that of my mother, sitting on the bed, crying.

I know now that by this choice I saved my life. I would

certainly have perished as my parents did if I had stayed behind. Instinctively, and borne out again by hindsight, I had made the right decision. And I truly know for sure that this is what my parents desired more than anything else in the world with all their heart—for me, at least, to survive.

And I survived, didn't I?

So why then have I been guilt ridden ever since? And as time goes by, ever more? Why am I tormented by remorse with an ever growing frequency and intensity?

It's bad enough to be orphaned at a relatively young age and to walk through life without your parents' love and care. It is even worse to be painfully reminded of their absence at every major turn of events—marriage, divorce, the birth of your children, their grandchildren, to miss their growing old, enabling you to reciprocate some of the care you had received yourself.

But worst of all is the unendurable knowledge of their final fate, the one you evaded yourself by that crucial choice made in 1942.

How often have I dreamed and nightmared about this their last journey in that overcrowded cattle train, no air, no food, no water, squeaking and groaning on and on, until that last final terminal stop.

That Train

The older I've become, the more clearly I can see it, smoking and whistling through that wintry landscape of my soul. Shadowy faces with hollow eyes glare at me behind small and barred openings, some unknown, some I should remember but try to forget, and the faces of the ones I loved.

And lately, more and more, I see another face behind those bars—a familiar face, one that has stared back at me from every mirror in my life, and that should have been on that train right from the outset.

And the whistles blow louder and louder, they scream and they shriek, and I do not need to wonder any more—they shriek for me.

THE ESCAPE

We had grown into quite a party when we departed: three couples and six singles, all in our twenties, with me the youngest one. We had all been provided with forged papers carrying false names, and we were headed for the midnight express from Brussels to Paris, where someone would wait for us at the station for further delivery.

I was wearing a workman's overall and a cap to top it off, all my visible black hair shaved away. I had no luggage at all and only God knows how I intended to manage for who knows how long with but a toothbrush and a shaver in my pocket.

We arrived at the Brussels station as late as possible, so as not to loiter around and attract unwanted attention. Keeping only eye contact without clinging together, we moved around in the hall, trying to act inconspicuously, fading away in the crowd. And the first trouble started right there when one of the girls exclaimed that she had lost the heel of her shoe.

Now this might not be judged such a dramatic event, except that there were five thousand dollars hidden in the heel. So we started frantically to look for it until she found out that the treasure had stayed put between the nails and had not fallen off.

By now it had become real late and we had to make a run for the train. We had planned to be seated in couples in such a way that one of each pair had good knowledge of French, but in the scramble the plan collapsed. Each one was now on his own.

The train was more than overcrowded. People were spilling out of the gangways, train doors were unable to close, and German soldiers were milling about the platform, shouting and cursing at the passengers.

I tried desperately to get in, to no avail, and the train started slowly to move. Then one German guard pushed me forcibly into the bulging mass and slammed the door hard on my back, still cursing and shouting, and I was on my way to Paris. If he only had known! Thanks anyway.

I had no idea if everybody had managed to enter and could not budge one inch to find out. Afterwards, when people left at some station, the situation eased, and I found a seat in the next compartment. One of us was sitting there already and we acknowledged each other silently, waiting for the oncoming border control.

In the dead of night the train stopped and German soldiers entered. They ordered everybody with suitcases outside and the others to prepare their identity papers.

We looked at each other, made an intuitive choice and got out with the luggage crowd. This proved to have been a good idea. Once outside in the dark night, the passengers were ordered to assemble their luggage at one lighted spot, then the valises were opened one by one, while the owners had to come forward and present their identity papers. At the end of the control, the passengers reclaimed their suitcases and the whole group reentered the train. As both of us possessed no luggage, we never had to present ourselves, nor show our papers. We just went out and in again with the crowd.

We were relieved when it was over and the train started to move again. So far so good. One break for us, a lucky one, an easy one, perhaps too easy. Because it was not always so easy to ride the escape trail to freedom, as many were picked off the trains. Stories abounded and here is one I know firsthand, which affected a former girlfriend of mine.

She and her parents were on a train in France trying to reach a neutral border. They occupied the same compartment but were seated separately, as they travelled under different false names each.

The Germans enter for control, people show their papers. The mother passes through, the daughter passes, too. The Germans examine the father's papers, look at him hard, suddenly smack his face, shouting: "You are a Jew." The father collapses and is dragged from the train.

Mother and daughter stay put, stifling all outward signs of emotion. Eventually, they make it to Switzerland and freedom.

By a grotesque twist of fate the father survived the death camps as a Capo, but was killed by the remaining inmates after their liberation.

What feelings of guilt the mother and the daughter must have been saddled with for life.

We arrived in Paris in the early morning hours. As I stepped out, I looked around cautiously and was greatly relieved to spot each one of our group in the crowd, pouring out of the train onto the platform. While slowly exiting out of the station, two men in civilian raincoats approached me, of all people, and started to search my clothes. They did not utter one word and I prayed silently, pokerfaced, that they would not ask any questions. My poor French was a source of danger. But apparently they found nothing warranting suspicious questions and I was able to join the others.

Indeed someone was waiting outside the station and we followed him in pairs and singles to some cheap rundown hotel where we stayed for a couple of days. We never left our rooms.

On arriving in Paris we did not know that the previous day a big *razzia* had taken place where tens of thousands of Jews were rounded up and brought to Drancy, later to be sent to Auschwitz. This is the same *razzia* shown in Joseph Losey's movie, *Mr. Klein*.

Mr. Robert Klein is a prosperous non-Jewish art dealer living comfortably with his wife and mistress in wartime Paris, making a good living from buying on the cheap valuable paintings from Jews on the run, until a fugitive Jewish namesake shakes the Gestapo off his trail by false-tracking them to Mr. Robert Klein, the gentile art dealer.

Our poor non-Jewish Mr. Klein tries everything to escape the unwanted and then so dangerous honour of belonging to the chosen people, but alàs, in vain. In the inevitable end he is caught in the net, sent to Drancy and then to Auschwitz, on that same day, the day of the great *razzia*—just one day before our arrival in Paris.

After a few days in Paris we made our next leap and took the train to Bordeaux, where we intended to cross by foot the demarcation line between occupied, and at that time, not-yet-occupied France. The voyage went off without incident and after a brief stay over we set out for the, until then, most important part of our flight, an all night hike through fields and woods into German-free Vichy territory.

It went off like a scene in a Hitchcock movie. At fixed points in the countryside were carts with their shafts pointing out the direction we had to take. Everything went according to plan, including the crossing we had to run through, one at a time, in perfect, albeit one-sided, coordination with the German patrol—they to the left, then one of us quickly to the right. Someone's sprained ankle was the only hitch, and when morning came we had made it. We had arrived in Vichy country, though capitulated and

German dominated, but at least it was not-yet-German occupied.

We took a train to Lyon and registered in a hotel in anticipation of further developments. I had handed over the money sewn in my pants to my family and received in return a small daily allowance for eating expenses. For a couple of weeks I idled away my days scanning the town, free at last from Gestapo terror.

Or so I thought.

One early morning at six o'clock the French police knocked at the door. Altogether four of our group were taken to a police station, while hundreds more were brought in from all parts of Lyon—all of them Jews, of all ages and sex. We were assembled in the inner courtyard, and even if we did not actually know then, as we know now, that the Vichy government had made a Jew-delivery deal with the Nazis, this premonition hereoff was perceived by all.

The pandominium was indescribable. The tears, the imploring, the pleas, grew by the hour.

Then the police started questioning and shifting, liberating people for all kinds of reasons—women, children, married couples, the aged, the sick, and those holding *good* foreign papers, backed by respectable embassies.

Mine were worthless. They were made out in Lyon, officially covering my stay there and the right to food ration cards. But they stated that I was a stateless refugee of Polish origin, which was like getting a guilty sentence in a murder trial. When I was led in for questioning, a civilian person was present and I felt that he was leading me on favourably, but to no avail.

At the end of the day, from the entire arrested multitude only twenty-seven young, male, foreign, unattached Jews were left. And I was one of them, the only one of

24

our group. We were locked up for the night in a rough, bare corridor with iron bars on all sides. For long hours we stood there screaming, rattling the bars, begging for release. It was one of the most despairing nights in my life.

In the morning we were loaded into a bus and transferred to Fort Barreaux, a huge prison in an isolated place in the mountains some four hours drive from Lyon. It consisted of a main camp and a special compartment for the more serious, hardcore criminals like murderers, etc. And lately also the present day outcasts of the new order—communists, homosexuals and Jews.

We were put up all together in a one-room, two-story barrack. The new day had inspired new courage. After the suspense and the despair at the police station, we now tried to convince each other—and ourselves—that though we were apparently imprisoned for the duration of the war, we were young and would survive.

The previous day, when still in the police courtyard in Lyon, I had received a food parcel from my relatives outside who apparently had remained free. Once in Fort Barreaux, I took it all out—several loaves of French bread and sausages—and shared the riches with all twenty-seven of us, everyone relishing his two slices. It made me feel good as if I were already living in a kibbutz somewhere in Palestine.

From the following day food parcels began to arrive for other inmates from their relatives and friends outside, whereas I received no more. And from the arrival of the first parcel the kibbutz act was done with and forgotten. Nobody even bothered to reciprocate with one single slice of bread, and I was hungry, as we all were, of course. Food was scarce and the little distributed could hardly be called French cuisine.

I was embittered and thought I had learned a valuable

lesson in real life. But not long afterwards I began to see it in another way. As events turned out, I was the only one saved out of the twenty-seven, the others disappearing soon into the holocaust.

The special compartment had a little courtyard where we mingled with the other inmates. There was one who assured everybody ready to listen of his innocence. He just happened to have an argument with his wife, happened to hold a knife in his hand, and she just happened to die from the "argumentation." Another one, a big fellow, volunteered to exchange my leftover bread coupons for real bread, and I never saw them again of course—the coupons nor the promised bread.

There were also two men, if I may designate them as such, who were dressed like women, with scarves, lipstick, and all. One was living with a permanent partner, the other was roaming about freely and unattached. That one, on the very morning of our arrival, wriggled up to me and cooed in a high pitched, "How are you, dear?" and I did not know how fast to flee to our barrack. I had never encountered anything like it, nor had I any real notion on the subject.

I tried to keep as much to myself as was possible in those circumstances, mostly lying on my second floor cot. I used to gaze through the little barred window at a patch of green meadow in the mountains far beyond the driveway leading up to the camp. I could make out a lone farm house set between big trees and daydreamed of living there, far out and safely hidden away from the turbulent times around and ahead.

Exactly one week after our arrival, all the other inmates except our group were transferred to the main camp. We were left alone in the special compartment, but not for long. Next morning, as I was lying on my cot and gazing, as usual, through the window and daydreaming about my patch of green, I saw the new prisoners coming in. They were climbing the driveway into the camp on foot, row after row, men, women, and children, within each row chained to each other, and all of them Jews. They were accompanied by a lot of French gendarmes, doing the dirty work. So the selections had become more severe by now.

For a week new groups kept on arriving and the compartment soon spilled over with human misery. Nobody knew what lay in store for us, but we went on hoping that we were just being interned until the war was over, which was already bad enough, but not mortal.

That same week the Dieppe landings by the allied forces took place and excited rumours spread through the camp. We all wanted very much to believe that this spelled the beginning of the invasion and liberation. But reality soon asserted itself. The allies retreated or were routed, and pictures of the many dead soldiers with their abandoned weaponry dashed all hopes of imminent salvation.

About a week later we were ordered out of the compartment, loaded into buses and departed in the direction of Lyon. Not far from it we turned and entered a big camp where thousands of Jews were concentrated and immediately upon arrival, while still in the buses, inmates told us that we were being transported to German-occupied France. The truth had come out at last. Nobody had an inkling of course of the real and final destination, but the transfer from Vichy's dirty hands to the German iron fist inspired nothing but evil premonitions.

We drove on to an office building for the inevitable registration procedure, leaving the buses and queueing up inside. Suddenly I heard my name called out repeatedly. A French official accompanied by two gendarmes spirited me outside the office and told me that I was free to leave the camp. The smiling guards walked me to the gate, and the gate opened up and I stepped outside floating somewhere in the clouds above, dazed from the bliss of being suddenly, unexpectedly, and in the nick of time, a free person again.

This surely was one of my finest hours.

It meant that my relatives were still free somewhere in Lyon and had succeeded in obtaining my release. The civilian present at my interrogation in the police courtyard had finally done it, against all odds, as I heard later. And at the very last moment, because, as I heard, too, on that same evening all the arrivals from Fort Barreaux were sent on to German-occupied France.

(Why me, why me again?)

With the few coins left in my pocket I took a bus to Lyon, and for lack of a better idea went to the same hotel I had been taken away from only two weeks earlier. To my great surprise, and our mutual joy, I found everybody present and free. They even occupied the same rooms as before, on the higher floors of the hotel. Apparently, the French police had not bothered that day to tire themselves out by climbing too many steps at the early hours of that morning. Blessed be their laziness.

Some had been compelled to compulsory residences in small towns, but had managed to make their way back to Lyon. We even had three new arrivals. A cousin, who was more or less the main organizer of our escape, had returned meanwhile to occupied Antwerpen and brought out his parents and brother, who was about my age. It was no small endeavour to go back, entering the lions' den, and going out again. It was a mixture of luck, money and great personal courage, with special emphasis on the last. Until his dying day, thirty years later, from a much too early heart failure, I have always admired him for that feat of daring.

Yet, the importance of the money factor cannot be underestimated. The harsh facts of life were, are, and remain that money makes the world go round. It certainly functions as a key agent for survival in perilous circumstances, and not even Scarlet Pimpernel could have done without it. It buys everything—food, shelter, false papers, tickets, officials, passeurs (who smuggle refugees through hostile borders), visas, connections—you just name it and money provides it.

I learned after the war that you could even buy false passports from certain Latin American consulates in favour of Jews already in German camps in occupied Europe. They would then be transferred to other and better camps, raising substantially their chances of survival.

When the situation deteriorated and it became dangerous to stay in hotels, we went into hiding *chez* Suzanne. She was a courageous non-Jewish French girl who had fallen in love with one of my cousins. She took all fifteen of us into her small two-bedroom apartment until we could find a way out.

The opportunity came soon enough, and not more than a week later we started our last leap to liberty—direction Switzerland. We would travel in two groups with the second one following only after safe arrival of the first. I was part of the first group consisting of the parents, sister, and younger brother of the organizer-cousin, another couple, Suzanne, and myself. Suzanne would see us through to the border, and then return for the second group one week later. Our destination was the town of Evian on the French side of Lake Geneve where a *passeur* would smuggle us by boat to the Swiss shore. If everything went according to plan, we would reach our freedom within twenty-four hours.

Through lack of time and in our hurry to flee from Vichy France, not all forged French identity papers were ready, and my uncle and aunt, the parents as I call them, travelled without them.

We set out in a taxi and after a couple of hours, about midway to Evian, we were halted by a French gendarme demanding our papers. Slowly, one after the other, we started to take them out while the policeman checked and returned the papers without saying a word. We all knew that the moment of truth would come with the turn of my uncle and aunt. They spoke no French at all and could not even mumble something about forgetfulness. And then it would be over.

When their turn came, my uncle started to fumble in his inner pocket as if looking for his-nonexisting-papers, and just when tension seemed to explode, the gendarme said quietly, *Ca suffit* (that's enough), got on his motorcycle and raced away.

I will never know why he let it go at that critical moment, but so many years later, from here to eternity, I still salute him in gratitude.

We arrived in Evian in the early hours of the evening. Opposite, on the northern side of the lake, was Geneve, shining brightly in the night. It was a fantastic sight. Here and all around us was darkness and gloom, and there lay that town lit up in splendour, illuminated as if the rest of Europe and its eternal blackout did not exist. Was it just a mirage, an illusion? Freedom was now so near, would we make that last stretch across the lake?

The inevitable hitch came when the *passeur* with the boat turned out to have been arrested a few days earlier.

But we managed to find another one who would smuggle us through the mountains, certainly a much more arduous journey than the shortcut trip by boat.

My uncle was an invalid who walked with a cane and a limp, a leftover from being trampled once by a mob. He must have been about fifty-five then. We had strong apprehensions on his ability to endure a mountain climb, but we were reassured by the *passeur*. It would not take more than two, three hours, he promised solemnly.

That very evening we left Evian by car, driving over winding, mountainous, steadily climbing roads. After two hours the car stopped and we got out. Three men stepped out of the shadows and told us to follow, while the car drove away.

But we did not budge. We were afraid. Too many stories had made the rounds among refugees of *passeurs* robbing and even killing their charges on lonely mountain slopes. But then, cutting through our arguments, my invalid uncle asserted leadership, admonishing us that there was no way back for us. We had no choices left anymore. As the truth sank in, we turned and started to climb, my cousin and myself taking up the rear to keep an eye for any eventuality.

As it turned out, our apprehensions were unfounded. The *passeurs* acted as they should and did what they could. Out of human compassion, no doubt, but for hard cash, too.

The promised two to three hours' climb turned into a full night and half a day of climbing—a true nightmare. The terrain was rough and difficult, there were no roads, and sometimes we had to traverse mountain streams, balancing on makeshift cut down trees. We climbed and climbed and then went on climbing more. Each time, when enquiring, we were reassured that it would not be too long now. And then we continued climbing. Finally we just stopped asking.

After some four hours my uncle could not walk anymore. He sat down weeping, beseeching us to abandon him then and there and go on without him. He would not stand in our way to freedom.

So his son and myself locked his shoulders between ourselves, supporting him while he limped with his cane, and we went on climbing.

After an hour more, my uncle could not stand on his feet any longer. So we carried him, one by the head, the other by the legs. He was a stocky, heavyset man, and after a while he felt like a mountain himself. The burden became unendurable. It was pure hell.

And yet we continued to climb on and on. It seems that we do not know the outer reaches of our strength, nor our capacity to tax it and endure in unusual circumstances. We really can move mountains.

At the early hours of the morning we arrived at a solitary chalet and collapsed inside, totally exhausted.

Then, after two hours of rest and refreshments, we set out for the final stretch—four more hours of climbing to the Swiss border at the very top of the mountain. This was the steepest part of all, and there was no physical possibility for my uncle to make it on foot, nor for us to carry him. So a horse with a sledge was prepared for him and we started out. We climbed very narrow steep paths, high-rising slopes on one side, deep precipices on the other. The *passeurs* were in front, then my uncle sitting on the sledge, his wife behind him, and then the rest of us, one after another.

My uncle sat straight as a tree, showing no signs of fear, even when the horse slipped and the sledge slid from side to side. After a couple of hours the terrain became so difficult that the sledge had to be abandoned My uncle then mounted the horse, riding as erect as a cowboy. The horse continued slipping, but my uncle did not seem to mind, as if he had been a rodeo rider all of his life.

The weather was warm and clear, and at last we reached the top of the mountain. The climb was over. It was high noon.

But we did not rest a minute. The *passeurs* with the horse retreated back into France, while Suzanne, wonderful, valiant Suzanne, stayed behind on the mountain top, watching us descend on the other side. We could see her head shrinking smaller and smaller as we plunged down on our backs and bottoms into free and neutral Switzerland.

SWITZERLAND

The descent was much easier than the climb and a lot faster, too. We just tumbled downwards, falling, rolling, gliding, not minding bruises and scratches from stones and shrubs, elated and cheering for having made it to Switzerland and to freedom. We did not know then that Swiss frontier guards were scanning the mountains with binoculars in order to catch border crossing refugees, who would then immediately be sent back to where they came from. You could be eligible for permanent internment only if you had succeeded to penetrate deep into the heart of the country.

Item

Months later, a fellow refugee in my labour camp got a phone call from his brother who had just crossed from France into a Swiss border cafe. The Belgian Embassy was called at once for help and protection, but to no avail. After several nerve-wrecking days of anxiety and uncertainty, he was informed that his brother had been expelled, never to be heard of again.

But ours was a lucky day. It was Sunday and a fiesta was being celebrated in a neighbouring village. Everybody attended, guards included, and security was apparently slack.

After we ended our tumble into the valley, bodies

bruised and clothes torn but happy as larks, we decided to rest a while. I left, found a deep hole at some distance and sat down to relieve myself. While sitting pretty, a man appeared, looked down at me, and walked on. I felt funny, but could do nothing than more of the same. A moment later a pretty young girl of about seventeen appeared, looked down at me, blushed, and, head held high in the sky, went on, too. Now I had become more than embarrassed, and before the whole village would parade by my hole, look down at me and go on, I finished my business and returned to the fold. And there they were, the father and the daughter, conversing with the others, informing us about the border guards, the binoculars and the village fiesta. They offered to help and took us to a nearby woods to hide and told us to wait until dark. They promised to fetch us during the night.

In the eyes of those good Swiss burghers, leading a pretty normal life in a neutral country, unperturbed by war and persecution, we must have been a pitiful sight. A shabby, miserable bunch of refugees, bruised, torn, and all. Which indeed we were, but with a slight but important difference: We were a happy bunch of shabby refugees.

Anyhow, they were fine people. They came by night as promised and led us to their chalet in the mountain village. They washed us, fed us, dressed us, and transformed our beggarly appearance into one of proper respectability. They put us up for the night and accompanied us next morning to the small railway station from where we departed for Zurich. A guard watched impassively as we kissed goodbyes, loudly calling each other "uncles," "aunts," and "cousins," acting out German-speaking Swiss citizens returning home from a family visit. The performance worked and late that night we arrived in Zurich.

A friend of my relatives waited at the railway station

and accommodated us in a fashionable hotel. For once I would enjoy a good night's sleep in a luxurious bed.

Next morning I presented myself at the Belgian Embassy as a refugee of Belgian nationality, which of course I was not. My parents had been Austrians from Polish origins, transformed into Germans by the Anschluss. Later, in 1940, all Jews were deprived of their German nationality, so we had become stateless persons. And that's what I was, then, actually. But in France I had already experienced the market value of statelessness as being next to nothing. I decided, therefore, to appropriate the Belgian nationality, for the rest of the war for my personal safety's sake, and to hand it back to the rightful owner when it was over. As a matter of fact, we all did likewise.

In that precarious September month of 1942 one could never know what the future had in store. Someday even the Swiss might come under German pressure to hand over Jews, for whatever dark purpose and destination. And who would be the first to go but the stateless ones.

So, after having paid due respect to the Belgian Embassy, I registered with the police as a Belgian refugee and could now not be expelled any more. I received my official permit to stay in Zurich until further notice, when I would be sent to one of the labour camps for young male refugees.

But then, as the group escape was over and we had found a safe haven in neutral Switzerland, the family responsibility was terminated. From now on I was on my own.

Later that evening, possessing no material means of my own, I entered a public park and spent the night on the green grass.

Such is the turn of life's wheel of fortune. One night you sleep between white clean sheets on a comfortable hotel bed, and the next on good mother earth. I confess preferring the first.

The following day I applied to the Red Cross and was allocated a bed in a long hall with many more bums like me. At least it was clean and included a warm meal each day.

The transition from where I came from to neutral Switzerland was incredible. I took long walks in Zurich and its surrounding areas, admiring the clean streets, delighting in the delicious pastries in the neat shops, never ceasing to wonder at the nightly illumination, as if there was no war going on. All those normal facets of life, that did not exist anymore for years in most of Europe.

When the second group arrived from Lyon a week later, our joint endeavour was brought to a safe conclusion. They travelled by the same road, climbed the same mountain, descended into the same valley, and were assisted by the same Swiss family on arrival, only this time it was prearranged. Suzanne had made the same journey again, and then this swell and brave girl had returned to Lyon. On arrival, the second group also registered as Belgian citizens—which, of course, they were not—and after a couple of weeks, the single males were sent to some of the several labour camps, mostly in the French-speaking part of Switzerland.

Many months of heavy manual labour were now to begin, none of us were accustomed to, many not able to. We built roads, cleared marshlands, hacked away at stones and trees, served as farm hands, all for board, bed, and the stingiest of compensation.

The Swiss treatment of refugees has often been compared to the behaviour of other neutral countries, and not exactly in their favour. In Sweden, for instance, refugees were also interned but not compelled to do forced labour, and most important of all, after crossing their borders, were never expelled anymore.

The hard work, poor pay and crowded barracks aside, conditions were not unreasonable. The food in the camp was sufficient, a canteen and a library added further to our needs, while the embassy provided a welcome supplement to our sparsely available pocket money.

On weekends we were at liberty to leave the camp, and finances permitting, mostly boarded the train to Lausanne. There we would turn loose on the bars and dancing halls, looking for girls. Being young and enclosed in all-male surroundings, the chase was our main occupation.

We were not looked upon favourably by the ordinary Swiss burgher, one of the reasons being understandable envy and anger for catching *their* girls. We were never invited into their homes or established any kind of social contact. They just did not like us, calling us names like *chaibe uslander* meaning damned foreigners. Naturally, they would have preferred full pocketed old-fashioned tourists crowding their now empty hotels.

Admittedly, sometimes we gave good cause for our unpopularity by occasional misbehaviour, though never anything of a violent nature. Listen to the following:

In the village near the camp was a bakery shop selling delicious pastries every Sunday morning. We would descend on the shop in droves and eat our fill from the display in the shop window. Then we would queue up at the counter, and pay—one only. After a while, the baker got suspicious and tried to get the better of us. He posted himself at the shop window and counted the number of pastries devoured while his wife handled the payments at the counter. And we would continue swallowing quantities at the shop window, and paying for only one at the cashier, there being no coordination possible in the crowded shop between the baker and his wife. Disgusting!

I too had my fair share in the chase. As a matter of fact, since their citizens dislike of us was mutual, their treatment of refugees nothing to write home about, and their eternal mountains slowly getting on my nerves, the girls are my fondest recollection of refugee life in Switzerland. I had several not so passionate and not so important relationships, and will not bore the reader but with some anecdotal fare.

One was no other than the first girl I encountered after plunging into Switzerland, albeit in a rather unusual position. One year later I remembered to send a thanksgiving letter to her family for their generous assistance to an unknown bunch of refugees. An exchange of letters then ensued with the girl, substance as well as signature growing gradually warmer with each letter, until she finally confessed love at first sight. Some sight! Apparently you can never tell what makes love tick.

Another one got me into prison, though not by any fault of hers. I had made a date in a nearby wood on a so-called restricted evening—one of the weekly three we were not allowed to leave camp. But I had been found out, and when I was sneaking back they were waiting for me. Next day, in the mess hall in front of everybody, the camp commander denounced my mean behaviour in harsh words and condemned me to one week of prison in a neighbouring village.

The first two days I was not permitted to leave the cell, not even to relieve myself. Apparently being a part of the punishment, this had to be done in an open pot not to be disposed of. Later conditions eased, and the guardian would even send me around the village to do his shopping. Anyhow, as a result of this incident I have been able to boast for the rest of my life about having done time like any other fellow criminal.

The only town we were not allowed to travel to was Geneve. It was the forbidden city of Switzerland. Funny, come to think of it. I had looked at inviting and brightly illuminated Geneve from blacked-out Evian in France, but could not reach it then by boat. And now, being interned in the country itself, could not go there either.

Meanwhile, the fortunes of war had turned around.

After years of bad tidings and disasters, the good news was coming in at last. First there was Stalingrad, then El Alamein, or maybe the other way around. Anyhow, the Nazis and their allies were being beaten and were now retreating both on the Russian front in Europe and on the northern shores of Africa. And then the Americans disembarked in Western Africa, and between Montgomery and the Yanks the fascist forces were thrown out of Africa altogether.

Those were glorious times. Each day we would march through the village in our funny earth-coloured rain capes to the sites of our labour, loudly singing well-known parade tunes, and cheering the fresh headlines displayed of the latest towns fallen to the allies. And when the Americans landed in Italy, captured Mussolini and that country capitulated, we exploded into outright hysterics. The news broadcast came through at mess time, and all of us started shouting, cheering, dancing, trampling, clapping plates on the table in a splitting orgy of uproar and joy. For a long time we were unable to calm down.

It would never be like that again. Despite the better tidings to come, not even D-Day, not even the surrender of Germany and later, Japan, could light again so much fire. Too many lives had been lost on the way, too many hidden facts had surfaced on the extermination of our dear ones, on the destruction of our people, to recapture that first frenzy in 1943.

Exuberance does not mix well with sorrow.

Not long after that memorable explosion of joy when Italy capitulated, I received bad tidings about my parents.

We had been corresponding all the time under false names and in veiled terms. We had to use assumed identities in our letters to and from the occupied countries in order not to volunteer unnecessary information which could be dangerous at both ends, as all letters were of course censored by the Germans. They even sent informers into our camps posing as refugees, two of those found out and expelled from my own barracks.

From those letters and hints in other relatives' letters, I had been informed on what had happened to them. For the remainder of 1942 they had been able to stay at the same old address, the shop and the apartment above. Once, my mother was arrested in the street, but my father succeeded in obtaining her release. In one of his last letters, while still free after the German defeat in Stalingrad, my father wrote about the recovered health of uncle Joe (Stalin) but added that it would come too late for them.

At the beginning of 1943 my mother was arrested again in the street, this time by big Bill, a notorious and infamous police officer who collaborated with the Gestapo in hunting Jews. But now my father's intervention attempt ended in his being arrested, too. They were sent first to one concentration camp, then, after some months, to another one, apparently a kind of transition camp.

From the first camp, they could not correspond, but from the second I received their one and last letter. They wrote that they were glad with the transfer, as the first camp had been very bad, and now in this one they could at least be together again. This was in July 1943.

I answered immediately, but my letter, addressed to that second camp, returned to me unopened. On the envelope was stamped in German: *transferred to the east, destination unknown.*

Obviously, that was the end.

Incoming mail was distributed at noon, during mess time, by calling out the names of the addressees. When I got my letter back, I left the camp and walked to the surrounding fields. I sat down on the ground for a long time and grieved for my mother and my father.

I did not know then what everyone knows now, neither the hidden meaning contained in that ominous caption on the envelope, nor the real destination of those transfers to the east. I had not heard yet of the Wannsee Conference and its decisions on the final solution of the Jewish problem. But instinct and foreboding told all there was to know.

After the war I was informed by the Red Cross that they were transported to the extermination camp Auschwitz in Poland and gassed on arrival.

THE ROAD BACK: PARIS

Soon after the liberation of Paris, the refugee stream reversed itself from Switzerland back into France and I joined the exodus with a group of other young Belgian males. We arrived in Paris and were lodged in a kind of transition house until our repatriation to Belgium, expected to be liberated soon, was possible.

As the outcome of the war was in no doubt anymore, I decided to go honest and disclose my not being a Belgian citizen, but a stateless person. This was a dumb mistake as I found out soon enough. Even in liberated France, to be stateless was still equal to being worthless—nothing. I came at once under pressure to leave the Belgian transition house.

As the war situation stagnated, I started shopping for work to support myself. The only jobs available to me were with the American Army, and because of my linguistic qualifications I had no difficulty at being contracted. But oh the trouble I encountered with the American security screening, the so-called G 2, an obligatory procedure before in fact starting to work! It appeared that their regulations allowed only allied nationalities to qualify, and the stateless = worthless equation asserted itself again. As a consequence I was not able to pass the American G 2 checks, intended actually to sort out and catch Nazis and their collaborators instead of their victims. How stupid bureaucracy can get!

They threw me out every time. Later on they got to know my face and picked me out of the line of applicants before even reaching the security officer. Once I succeeded in outsmarting them and started working in one of their units as chief of forty French girl workers. I passed quite an interesting day but that same evening I was called to the office and dismissed. It had happened again, the G 2 had intervened.

Meanwhile, the pressure to leave the transition house mounted, but I had nowhere to go, no means of support, and no job to be found.

One evening I went to the movies, showing Berthold Brecht's *Beggars Opera*. I went to bed on my second floor cot in the big sleeping hall, musing and dreaming about Jack the Knife. As usual, both my suitcases with all my belongings, which did not amount to much anyway, were standing next to the cot on either side. The clothes I had worn that day were laid out on one of the valises.

I woke up next morning, looked to the left and there was nothing, looked to the right and there was nothing either. Everything was gone, evidently stolen during the night. Even the clothes from my back. I was left in my pyjamas.

Particularly painful was the loss of my parents' letters, including the last envelope with the fateful caption on which I had shed many a tear.

Now I became really desperate. Though the war was not over yet, the propitious outcome was assured. The good guys had licked the bad guys and, personally, I myself had escaped the holocaust intended for me, too. And yet, here I lay on some bare cot in free Paree, no clothes on my back, nowhere to go, no money to live on, and no job to be had. And ordered to leave even that miserable wooden cot. I really did not know what to do next. The last straw I could think of was borrowing a suit and sending a cable to relatives in New York, pleading for help. Then

I changed back into my pyjamas, returned the suit, lay down on my cot and did not get up anymore.

But when my plea was answered, several weeks and a fistful of dollars later, I no longer needed them.

After three days spent on the cot, an enquiry reached me from an American hospital I had previously applied to and been accepted by. I was asked why I did not present myself at the job. They needed me. I explained to the officer in charge that I could not get the required G 2 clearance and the stupid reason why not. He was silent for a moment and then told me to come over right away. He would take care personally of those "idiots of the G 2." And so I started my job in a borrowed suit, and in no time was able to leave that wretched house and support myself independently and properly.

And then I met Madeleine.

She was a secretary at the hospital and I fell in love with her at first sight. She was not beautiful, not even what you might call pretty. But she had a nice open face and a figure to match. And above all, she had that special French charm—so hard to define, all female, entirely dedicated to matters of the heart. Her parents had been executed by the Germans for hiding a downed American pilot, so she was an orphan and an only child, too.

I courted her, she put me off for a while, I had my time of anguish, but in the end I went to live with her in her parents' suburban home. Our relationship ripened and deepened, and became my first truly mature love affair, not anything like those hanky panky Swiss adventures. We stayed together for quite a time, long after the war was over and and the world became free again.

I had nowhere to go back to anyway. She was my only attachment left. Both being war orphans, we found

45

support and solace in each other's arms. We never discussed the future, hers, mine, or ours. Once, at the beginning, she told me about a fiancé who had been sent to Germany and had never returned. But she did not mention him again.

We worked and dined and loved and were happy together. Our lovemaking was frantic, as if we had to make up for lost time in the past or in the future.

We were immersed in each other and I became more and more attached to Paris. As my French had become impeccable, I was well on my way in turning into a real Parisian.

But nothing lasts forever.

As time went by, I lay awake some nights pondering my future—where I wanted to live and where I should take roots, ultimately.

The war was over and the allies had won. But European Jewry had lost, all six million of them. They had been helplessly exterminated like cockroaches, my own parents included. And nobody, nobody had come to their rescue.

A new struggle was now in the offing. The Jews of Palestine and those willing to join them were about to take on everyone standing in their way—violent Arab resistance and the entire obstructing British Empire, in an all-out effort to achieve independence. At that particular moment of history, of a Jewish fight after Jewish plight, world opinion and the newly founded United Nations might just conceivably back Jewish rights. It was now or never.

I had heard the call. I had to go and do my bit. It was but the logical continuance of my past, the raison d'etre of my personal survival in the present, and the only future I could live with.

Time out with Madeleine was over.

THE ROAD BACK: ANTWERPEN

First I had myself repatriated to Antwerpen. I had to disengage myself from the past, all that had been, and was no more. I had to confront the many faces missing and bid farewell to those few who were left.

On the very first day of my arrival in Antwerpen I felt compelled to approach and face the home I had left in the summer of 1942, which seemed like only yesterday and yet also ages ago. Standing there in the middle of the street, I looked at our house.

Our store was a coffee shop now. A couple of elderly people sat quietly at a table, sipping their drinks. Nobody moved, no sound was heard, while I was screaming inside myself. No, this was all a fake, a cover up. It just had to be. This was *our* shop. My father was inside folding trousers and my mother upstairs cooking.

As I stood there in the grip of my emotions, the kitchen window on the first floor opened and a strange woman's face stared at me. I looked back and slowly reality began to sink in. This was no stage set. This coffee shop and the people inside were real, actually the only real ones around. The only stranger on the scene, the one not belonging, was me. My father and mother were nothing but memories in my mind, their physical shapes blotted out of existence as fluffs of red smoke through burning chimneys in far away lands years ago.

While still standing there I heard an astonished voice shouting at me: "Hey, you are not dead?"

I turned round and there was our neighbour standing in front of her butcher shop. I went inside to find out if she had some useful information, which she did not. But unasked for, she told me the story of our cat.

For the last couple of years we had kept a reddish-coloured kitten, not very orginally called Reddie. She was as playful as they come, slept in my bed when nobody was looking, and our favourite game, when I came home from school, was my playing with the letter flap from the outside with Reddie running wildly, trying to catch my fingers.

When the end came she was left behind, alone in the closed house. For two weeks the butcher's wife saw and heard her meowing at the windows, until she could not stand it anymore, broke the glass, and took the cat into her shop. But our starved and weakened Reddie would not or could not take in any food and died in a matter of hours.

I know, I know, Reddie was just an animal. And what matters the miserable end of one lost kitten when measured against the countless human tragedies of those cruel times, when life was cheap, and when you were not supposed to waste your tears on minor side shows?

But I do. One of the skeletons still rattling in my private war cabinet of horrors is our poor little Reddie, suddenly left alone in an empty and closed house. Nor can I erase the image of that moustached snout, pressed at the window panes, whining and wailing day after day until she finally passed away.

At first I went to live with remaining relatives, and later shared a room with a friend. He was one of our group who intended to found a kibbutz after the war. All four male members had survived, but only one of the girls. We renewed our plans and also participated in reviving the Zionist movement. The main task was now to move pioneers to Palestine as fast and as many as possible. Time was running out and the moment of truth was near. For this purpose specially trained envoys had been sent by the Jewish underground in Palestine who formed the nucleus of the approaching struggle. The Jewish Brigade, comprised of Jewish volunteers from Palestine, while officially part of the British Army of occupation, supplied the logistics: uniforms, lorries, communications, etc., all clandestinely, of course.

A web was spread all over Europe. Safety houses were set up, mostly lonely country houses in remote places. Some were located on the crossroads leading southwards, others on the shores of the Mediterranean, mainly in France and Italy. Ships were chartered, adapted to mass transportation, and set out inconspiciously to the designated departure sites.

This mass movement of illegal Jewish emigration to Palestine was set in motion on a grand scale. Jews were being assembled and guided through Europe's borders southwards by all available means—the facilities of the Jewish Brigade, helpful sympathisers, through bribes, cunning, in short, by hook and by crook. Ultimately, in the dead of night, they would board the shaky vessels to more than overcrowding, defy the British blockade, and sail their charges to the Promised Land.

This exodus is one of the magnificent sagas of modern times and I waited now for my turn to participate in it.

Meanwhile I had been corresponding with Madeleine and longed to meet her once again before my departure. So one day I joined friends travelling to Paris by car. As I had no travel papers of any kind, I showed the guards at the French border my former gate entrance pass to the American Hospital with the caption: *laisser passer*. They looked at it and did just that.

I had not divulged my visit in advance, wanting to

keep my arrival as a surprise. As I went along towards her house, a man walked slowly in front of me and I knew instinctively that he was her former fiancé coming home from German exile. Later it turned out to be true and I cannot offer any explanation for this remarkable flash of intuition, nor for the odd coincidence of both of us arriving at exactly the same time.

And so poor Madeleine had to part from two lovers, one week after the other. They talked and talked for hours, while I waited it out discreetly in another room. But in the end she sent him away. And a couple of days later, it was my turn to leave. This was our last farewell, our final break.

It is perhaps strange that I never attempted to influence Madeleine to join me. I think that her being gentile and French restrained me. But whatever the reason, I did not. Fundamentally, my road was not hers to travel, my load not hers to bear.

After a week of happiness mixed with sadness, I returned to Antwerpen. We would never see each other again, nor engage in any correspondence ever. But I have not forgotten her, and wonder sometimes what might have become of my first love. And who knows, the wondering might even be mutual, no?

Very soon thereafter my number came up, and I set out by underground to Palestine.

UNDERGROUND TO PALESTINE

So I took again to my illegal frontier crossing habit, though I sincerely hoped it would be for the last time. And this once it was done by the courtesy of his Majesty the King. Everything—uniforms, transportation, travel documents were all provided by the British Army, albeit without their knowledge and consent, of course. And furthermore, ironically enough, it was directed ultimately at crossing borders thousands of miles away guarded by the very same British troops!

After staying for a day in a safe house—a lovely mansion in a vast park—we ended up near a small harbour not far from Marseille in another big manor laid out in splendid scenic settings. Here we had to wait until the arrival of the other fellow travellers and of the ship that would carry us to our destination.

I spent quite a few pleasant weeks there and would have occasion to remember them with nostalgia during the sea voyage, certainly during the second part of it. I had befriended a nice, serious non-Jewish French girl, who for some idealistic reason had decided to join a kibbutz in Palestine. We strolled and talked a lot and, owing to our knowledge of the French language, had occasion to make several trips to Marseille shopping for the otherwise strictly guarded compounds. No love affair, though. That was to be had abundantly at the camp, where love and sex were easy commodities then.

The site became ever more crowded as scores of young Jews arrived each day, mostly being survivors from the death camps. They were a tough breed, cynical, undisciplined, out to make up for lost time, and carelessly disposing of the dos and don'ts presumably attached to normal social behaviour. When emerging from hell, you just don't give a damn about these niceties anymore.

The only respect even the rowdiest showed was towards the camp commanders, the envoys of the Hagana, the Jewish underground movement in Palestine. They were native born and Hebrew-speaking, sometimes wearing uniforms of the Jewish Brigade, sometimes civilian clothes. They assumed natural leadership with quiet, inconspicious authority, generally not interfering or mixing with the crowd, appearing and leaving as they saw fit.

The site itself was noisy and unruly, mostly in lively commotion by day and night. There were discussions and dances, fun and fights, chasing and lovemaking as young people would act everywhere, only more intensely so, straightforward, without social conventions, no beating about the bush. And a lot of bush, I may say!

In due course, probably only a few years later, normalisation would set in. All those rowdies would settle down to the ordinary aspects of life—marriage, raising kids, going to work every bloody morning, railing against the stupid government—all that we take for granted in regular circumstances.

But the nightmares stay on forever.

There was that youngster for instance, who had witnessed his father being clubbed to death right next to him in an Auschwitz line. During daytime he was as cheerful and playful as anyone else. But some nights he would wake up screaming, and a pretty girl, always the same, would come over and comfort him back to sleep. But they did not marry and live happily every after as the soaps try to make-believe us. They split on arrival in Palestine, and a couple of years later, when he was drafted into the army in the War of Independence, he shot himself.

One night, our numbers already reaching eleven hundred, we were loaded into trucks and drove to Sète, a small harbour in the south of France. The long-awaited moment had arrived, at last. We embarked in total darkness, silently and orderly, into the waiting vessel for the illegal journey back to our legal homeland.

All had been well prepared and organised. Rows of bunks had been built four high in various holds, and everyone was allocated his or her place. There was enough food and water, and during the first week nothing very special occurred. I was made head of a group guarding the drinking water, and but for bouts of seasickness and being packed like sardines, we were happily anticipating the arrival at our destination, speculating if we would succeed in landing undetected.

Also on board was an American journalist by the name of I. F. Stone, who intended to chronicle this modern exodus of the Jews. In due time he would publish a book called *Underground to Palestine*, describing our journey in great detail, reporting the events, as well as the people aboard. On arrival he would produce his American passport and return to the United States, serving the Zionist cause by the impact of his personal account.

There was big Rudy, for instance. He was a towering figure of a man who had allegedly been a Capo in Auschwitz, and now broke iron chains to entertain his fellow travellers. Many more are described by Stone. My non-Jewish girl friend is mentioned in one of the pages, and even our group is reported, though not cautious me, luckily.

From time to time, when passing dangerously close

to other ships, we had to descend and hide in the holds in order not to arouse unwanted suspicions. In our cat-and-mouse game with the British Navy we did not intend to volunteer advance information on illegal blockade busters.

Except for those bouts in the holds, we would pass the days on the decks, milling around in high spirits. Aside from the discomforts of overcrowding, we might as well have been on a Mediterranean cruise.

On the seventh day of our journey, about one more day from our destination, the ship stopped in midsea. We appeared to have a *rendezvous* there with a second ship which would take us over for the last stretch, running the British blockade. We were ordered to pack and be ready.

Then self-made immigration certificates were distributed, called "Permits to enter Eretz-Israel (Palestine)." They were printed in Hebrew on one side, English on the other, and issued at Naples by the "representative of the Jewish Community for the repatriation to Eretz Israel," signed by one Rabbi Moshe Ben Maimon, alluding to a famous Jewish philosopher in the Middle Ages, also known as Maimonides.

Four authorities were cited as justification for qualifying for repatriation: two verses, one each from the prophets Isaiah and Ezekiel, the Balfour Declaration of November 1917, and the Mandate for Palestine bestowed on England by the League of Nations for the express purpose of promoting and establishing a Jewish homeland in Palestine.

The certificates were even numbered to make them look ostensibly more official. Mine was numbered 13629. Try to find me out by it! No chance as there does not exist any solid registration. Anyhow, the name written on it is not even my real name anymore.

I still preserve the memento.

The second ship turned out to be a small Turkish freighter of only 250 tons, the *Akbel*, much smaller than our first ship. When the captain perceived the amount of passengers he had to carry, he balked and refused. And not without good cause, as we were to find out soon enough. But in the end, he was persuaded with the help of a gun.

Already the transfer of the passengers did not proceed smoothly. First they tried to moor the *Akbel* next to our ship, but that did not work out because of the gales. So we had to be transshipped by using two small lifeboats and a motor launch, women first, then the men, and then the luggage. The completion hereof would take long and dangerous hours.

I was assigned to a group staying behind on the first ship in order to assist people to descend into the boats, and later to transship all the luggage. It was a very hot July day, so I worked stripped to the waist in nothing but bathing trunks and a pair of sandals.

For long hours the three little boats traveled to and fro between the ships, and at last all the passengers were on the *Akbel*. Then, when part of the luggage had yet to be transferred, a British plane appeared in the sky, spotted us, dived, flew over and around several times, and disappeared.

We knew we had been detected. Seen from above, the overcrowded decks of the *Akbel*, so near to Palestine, revealed the story loud and clear: illegal Jewish immigrants on their way to the promised land.

So we halted at once the transfer of the remaining luggage and I joined the *Akbel* with the last boat trip. And then, while our first ship sailed away at full speed to the west, the *Akbel*, now renamed *Beria*, displayed the Jewish national flag and turned to the east, headed for Palestine.

And not one hour later a British warship appeared at the horizon, looming ever larger and more menacing between ourselves and our intended destination.

My own luggage turned out later to be with those we had to leave behind. Renamed *Haganah,* our first ship returned a month later from a Rumanian port with another 1500 illegal immigrants. They were seized by the British and interned in the British detention camp at Atlith in Palestine when I, too, was still detained there. Although part of the abandoned luggage was recovered, mine was not. Again, as in Paris not so long ago, I was left with nothing on my back. But instead of the Paris pyjama, I had now, very appropriately, bathing trunks to start my new life with. And as history seems to repeat itself, the only loss I really cared for, as in Paris, was a memento from my parents, a small golden wrist watch my father had once bought for my mother and was somehow returned to me after the war. Clothes are really nothing, as the boy said to the emperor. They serve no other purpose than to be worn and thrown away.

The next two days and two nights spent on the *Akbel* are easily the worst physical ordeal I ever had to endure in my whole life. It was much worse even than the climb to reach neutral Switzerland. In later years, the mystical streak in my nature would come to regard those forty-eight hours as my own private personal birth pains for attaining the promised land. But that thought was no solace to me then and there.

Stone, in describing those days and nights in great detail, uses terms like inferno and concentration camp conditions. But he was a "privileged character" on board, as he readily admits. When I read in his book about his cups of tea with the captain, the big cans of drinking water "though warm and stale," the buckets of seawater thrown over him to cool off, and most of all the precious little time he spent, though voluntary, for "nearly two hours," in the infernal engine hole, I cannot but envy his privileged position.

There simply was no room on little *Akbel* for so many people. If on the first ship we thought we were packed like sardines, this much smaller boat was totally crammed, crawling with people, squatting on every conceivable and inconceivable spare foot of space. There was no room at all to move about and lie down. Just imagine bunches of grapes, with grapes being people.

But the vast majority crammed on the deck were the lucky ones. Worst of all was the engine hold. This hold had to be occupied fully all the time, otherwise the boat could not move, which was slow and difficult enough, anyway.

Inside the hold it was pure hell. No other description fits that scene. Here was Dante's inferno in real life.

It was dark inside but for an eerie glow emanating from the engines. The stench was sickening, the noise deafening, and the overcrowding indescribable. But worst of all was the terrible heat and unbearable thirst, as we had received no water at all. When leaving the first ship a lunch bag was handed out containing a sandwich and a bar of chocolate, of all things, which turned out to be our entire nourishment for the following two days and nights. But what is the pain of hunger compared to the hell of thirst in those hot sub-tropical July days, dumped in that infernal hole.

In principle the hold should have to be occupied by everybody for short periods in orderly turns, but in reality I sat in that hole for nearly all the time.

After my first hours on deck I descended into the hold when my turn came. At first there was still some order, with big Rudi playing capo all over again, handling the circulation by allowing the hold people to go up only when new replacements came down. But later even he lost control and could not force anyone down anymore, and so I stayed there for more than forty hours until the end.

Stone, when describing his short stay in the hold, points at those "who may very well have been there in the darkest far corners since they came on board, too utterly spent to move."

Nice to meet you, Mr. Stone!

The boat groaned under the heavy load it could scarcely carry. For long periods it was not able to move at all and who knows what might have happened. Desperate pleas were shouted by loudspeakers over the sea to the British cruiser shadowing us, pleading to tow us to Haifa, or at least supply us with drinking water. But all our supplications were left unanswered and unheeded by those nice English gentlemen. Even the water. So much for perfidious Albion.

Rumours spread that an elderly person had succumbed to exhaustion and was secretly thrown overboard, but this was never confirmed.

I suppose that the transfer scheme to a boat of such small a size for so many people was based on the assumption that we would not have to endure it for more than approximately one day, being the nautical distance from our meeting place at sea to Palestine. After reading Stone's account I understand now that the Turkish captain, who did not want to take on such a multitude in the first place, had sailed for one whole day in the wrong direction. Furthermore, because of the overload, the boat stopped all the time, and even when succeeding to sail could not make normal speed.

Otherwise, it would have been quite an irresponsible

act from the Jewish Agency, to say the least, as a major disaster might have occurred. After all, we did not flee death camps anymore to warrant such risks!

But even when minutes seem like hours, and hours like eternity, time flows on, and on the early morning of the third day, surrounded by British warships, we reached the shores of Palestine. We were as yet outside the territorial waters, but the panoramic sights of Haifa, set against the green slopes of Mount Carmel, cleared slowly out of the morning mist. It was the most wonderful sight I ever saw in my life.

I had crawled out of the hole, totally dried up and spent from thirst and sheer exhaustion. But like everyone else I shouted and cheered and wept. The son of a famous cantor started a well known song about Jerusalem and we all listened in silence. Then our Haganah commander appeared on the bridge, flanked by others so the British would not be able to spot him with their binoculars. He took his leave from us requesting not to be recognized any more but to be ignored. Indeed, I never saw him again.

I heard later that secret compartments had been installed in the illegal ships for hiding those Haganah people. On arrival, after everyone had been taken off the ship, they were fetched by small boats during the night. And so they would never be caught, and in time would return to the network in Europe to continue the good work.

Now the British came on board and towed us into the harbour. Then a Jewish official appeared and started the usual welcome speech, but the poor fellow was silenced by our shouts for water and fled in a hurry.

Then a boat moored alongside and filled the only water tank on deck, possessing but one single tap. Can you imagine what is going to happen when one tap has to quench the thirst of eleven hundred dried out throats?!

The pandemonium was indescribable, as everybody started a free-for-all for one single cup of cool water. What a spectacle we must have presented for the benefit of those onlooking English gentlemen who so haughtily had ignored our desperate pleas when at sea. Even now I would still like to wipe the smirk from their arrogant faces. I am astonished that Stone does not mention this scene in his book. Perhaps he had left ship by this time.

But I do report it, and exhausted as we all were, not in the least myself, our group banded together and fought it out until each one, the girls too, had drunk his or her cup of water.

It was my first one after forty-eight hours and the best one of my entire life.

For several weeks after arrival I was not able to walk normally, only slowly and shakily like an old man. So exhausted had I become. And for several more months I would always keep a full canteen of water at my side. So scared had I become of ever having to endure thirst again.

But I had reached Palestine.

It was July 1946.

THE EXECUTION

Since that arduous voyage of the redeemed to their promised land, many turbulent years have passed, and in their course I've become an old man, living alone with a dog.

We found safe haven all right when disembarking on the shores of our new-old homeland, only to become engulfed once again in a seemingly endless collective destiny of strife and struggle. And I was part of it all. I could tell quite interesting stories about my subsequent experiences and adventures. However, I will not stray from the main theme of these chronicles: remorse and revenge. So a few general outlines will have to suffice.

My endeavours to found a new kibbutz turned into a failure, though it came very close to succeeding. Soon after arrival I started to roam the country for likeminded volunteers, eventually settling down in an established kibbutz for preparatory agricultural training. Meanwhile, a steady stream of new arrivals joined us straight from the immigrant ships. We grew bigger and stronger—to about one hundred young pioneers—and were but a few weeks away from being settled independently on our own piece of land.

And then, all of a sudden, the whole thing fell apart at the seams. It began with three single girls male-attracted away to another group of young settlers. But then desertions spread like the plague, and in no time nobody was left to pioneer with anymore. So that was the end of the affair, a dream come untrue.

I made several new starts, wandering here, roving there, attempting various trades and professions, until at last I found my niche within a large company, spreading its tentacles over many parts of the globe.

I married, divorced, remarried, and became an early widower. In time I climbed the executive ladder, and then, one fateful afternoon, the company phone rang. At the other end was the boss.

He invited me for a private lunch and a quiet chat, and after the small talk came quickly to the point: How would I feel about it if he offered me to assume responsibility for the Antwerpen-centered operations, and yes, I said, yes, and soon thereafter took off for the city of my youth, the city I had left nearly forty years ago.

I swear to God almighty that when accepting the assignment I had no other intentions in my mind than doing my job to the best of my abilities. At least consciously. But once back in town, wandering those familiar streets, everything I had buried for so many years surfaced with a vengeance. As if a tightly locked door had suddenly sprung wide open.

Many a twilight hour I would sneak up discreetly to our former home, and stand there, unobserved, brooding silently, drowning helplessly and irreversibly in the haunting images of the past. As time passed, it became the central focus of my existence, although I took great care to conceal any outward signs of my emotions. I continued fulfilling the obligations and exigencies of my job; however, it had regressed into the outside facade of my inner turmoil. While I pretended that the show went on as before, the real me boiled with pent-up rage.

Then I happened to come across an article about certain events from long ago, mentioning a name long suppressed and forgotten. And then, suddenly, while shockwaves of excitement flushed my body, the answer to those disturbing, lifelong why-me questions flashed through my mind. At long last it became clear to me. I knew now, and perhaps had known unconsciously all along, why I had been left to survive—why I had not been on that far-away and long-ago train with its whistles screaming into the night.

A cold calmness settled over me. I made a few quiet investigations. I thought it over for a long time, considering all aspects, coolly, methodically. At the end I decided to wait patiently and bide my time until the right moment would arrive. And I knew exactly when that would be. Meanwhile I continued the acting performance as if nothing had happened, and eventually, upon termination of my contracted stay, packed my belongings, bid my farewells, left the country, and returned home.

Not more than one week after my "final" departure I returned incognito for the execution.

Yes, reader. An old man, beset by guilt and obsessed with vengeance, came back to commit the proverbial perfect crime in the name of supreme, though private, justice.

When that bastard snatched my mother away in that street back in 1943, he caused a chain of misery, leading to my parents' violent end, by choking. But unknown to him, with that same dastardly act he triggered another sequence of events, leading ultimately, nearly fifty years later, to his own execution. By choking, of course.

How sweet is retribution.

I landed in a neighboring country and proceeded to Belgium by train. There was no border control of any kind. I checked into a modest hotel under an assumed name, not actually having to show my passport, as is quite customary nowadays. Just for the poetic touch of it, I registered under an anagram for *avenger*. I never left my room but for that one night of vengeance and departed from Belgium the morning after, the same way I had arrived. I had encountered no one, and nobody will ever be able to prove I had been in the country at all. Amazing, how easy an undetectible murder can be carried out.

Everything went according to plan, nothing went wrong that might have gone wrong, as usually happens in imaginary tales or movies.

There was not nor is there any personal connection to link me with the victim. I left no fingerprints, no traces, no explanatory notes.

As a matter of fact, the apparent senselessness of it was part of my revenge, reflecting the senselessness of the original sin, which in turn might have been the only clue for a clever investigator, albeit farfetched. I was pretty sure, however, that the police would not press the case in the direction of war related motives, in view of their own record of wartime collaboration. They could hardly be expected to point an accusing finger at themselves.

I spare the reader the sordid details of the killing, disclosing only that I went through it with the cold determination and detachment of a preset mechanical robot. Only afterwards, in some dark corner of a dimly lit alley, I began to shake and sob and vomit. But after a while I calmed down and returned to the hotel, serenely asking for my key. It was all over and done with.

I have always realised of course, that he had been no more than a small, insignificant bolt in that vast killing machine created for the extinction of the Jews.

But so was I. Within the array of penalising institutions created for the express purpose of seizing and punishing those countless criminals of the holocaust, I have been but a small, insignificant bolt myself.

A lonely self-appointed avenger, meting out his own private justice on one cowardly bastard in one single act of revenge for one foul deed committed long, long ago.

EPILOGUE

That fellow is a lunatic! Bumping off an old man just for arresting an ill-starred as well as yellow-starred woman so many years ago, however deplorable the deed itself!

That's what you have been thinking, isn't it? And you know, you may perhaps be right, too. And all apparently normal people will heartily and righteously agree with you.

But then, is it really so? It is really me who is the madman and not you, that so-called normal person? For once in that ordinary normal life of yours I challenge you to follow my reasoning and try to see it my way. For this once only, leave behind the wining and the dining, the well-stacked tables, the glittering ballrooms; switch off the music, even if the orchestra is beautiful. For once, leave your wonderful shapes frozen stiff and suspended right in the middle of the dance—take my hand and come with me.

Come with me to hell on earth.

No fairy tales of would-be vampires or wooden Frankensteins, no horror shows on silver screens you always love to flock to. Come with me to scenes of real life as they occurred not so long ago, day after day, night after night, in the heart of Europe at the core of our western civilisation—*excusez le mot.*

And please be silent, too, so you will be able not only to see the sights, but hear the noises, smell the stench, feel the pain, experience the anguish and the shock, the humiliation and the terror and the mortal fright, which were oh-so-normal at that time in this our blessed twentieth century.

What? You try to back out already? Run away to your wonderful shapes and marbeled floors and reserved tables? And you ain't even seen nothing yet?

Too late now, poor little frightened normal person. I'm holding on to your hand and won't let you go no more. Just bite your lips, squeeze my fingers until I'll set you free again in but a couple of lousy minutes. That's a promise. So here we go.

Look at that child over there, lying and crying on his wooden cot. They just brought him back from an important scientific experiment by the Herr Doktor. He had another child's hunchback transplanted upon this little fellow.

Fery interesting and exciting, nein?

His wounds are already infested and he will die in a couple of days.

But fe hafe at least those days, nein?

Meanwhile, the child lies on his stomach, whimpering away his last days on good mother earth.

Do you hear him, normal person? Did anyone in this, your normal world ever see his tears and hear his cries during fifty years of indifferent silence?

Now come with me and join that line and push inside when the doors are closed and the sizzling starts and the naked people realise that they are going to be choked to their deaths.

How long does it take from that first twist of terror

till that last rattling gasp? How long or how short is eternity?

Do you hear their cries for their fathers and their mammas, for their sons and for their daughters; do you hear them cry out for their God? Oh God, did you ever hear the cries of your children, why did you never hear the cries of your children? Where have you been, oh God, when the fires were lit and your people were burned on the stakes . . .

I can feel your hand now, desperately tearing at mine, wildly struggling to escape. But I cannot let you go, not yet. Give me five minutes more just to ponder on the following:

Those were not, I repeat, not, scenes from Dante's inferno. He could not have imagined them. I know it's hard to realise, but those were real happenings that had befallen millions of real people of real flesh and substance. However, it could never have been carried out without the active participation of tens of thousands of willing accomplices. From detached planners in distant offices to vile traitors and violent body snatchers and indifferent transporters and willing helpers and dutiful guards to the subhuman butchers at the factories of death. Moreover, they could never have happened without the passive collusion of millions of uniform bearers, fighting and conquering and providing the time, space, opportunity and protection for it all to occur.

So what happened when it was all over, when the Reich of a thousand years came tumbling down, when the secret of the final solution became public knowledge?

Did the victors mete out appropriate punishment for those enormous crimes? Were all, or nearly all, or even most of those murderers and their helpers, patronisers and protectors apprehended and brought to trial? Has justice been done?

The answer is unequivocally clear: No, it has not. Justice has not been done.

Only a miserable sprinkling of those active tens of thousands have been caught, even less tried and convicted. Against one imprisoned Barbie doll and one hanged Eichmann—even his arrest was legally illegal—many thousands have managed to live out their earthly lives peacefully and undisturbed.

Can anyone really doubt that the Herr Doktor could not have been found out and seized and tried and punished, if they had cared enough and dedicated concerted efforts towards that end?

Let's admit it. Except for a few "weirdoes" like the Klarfelds and Wiesenthal, the great majority of all those normal persons wanted nothing else than not to be bothered any more and just forget about it all.

So justice has not been done.

Now I ask you, should such behaviour be the proper procedure in view of such horrors performed? Is not even the tiniest act of justice, even when meted out privately and illegally, better and morally preferable than no justice at all? If that is the only choice available?

Answer me!

Do I hear the echo of your voice, faintly, far away . . . mumbling . . . what?

ANSWER ME, DAMMIT!

It's gone now. I cannot hear you anymore. You must have succeeded, at last, to tear yourself away and run. Coward!

So back you are in your wonderful shapes on the marbled floors at your well-stacked tables. Slowly, the music starts up again. A little squeaky, at first, then ever more harmoniously. The dancers start moving again, awkwardly at first, then quicker and quicker, circling wildly around each other.

The orchestra is beautiful.